ScATTEREd

LI
PI

100-word stories

By

Wayne Fenlon

Scattered Little Pieces

First Edition August 2020

Cover photo by Wayne Fenlon

ISBN: 9798679312630

For Liz, Joe and Katie.

THE RESTAURANT

I'm trying to get on with my life, but I can't break this god-awful habit of throwing up.

Maybe I shouldn't have come to this restaurant: all these people stuffing their faces, giving me sneaky glances and talking about disease.

I pretend to look out the window, see my unrecognisable reflection: thin arms and legs, a huge bloated stomach.

Do people understand the amount of shit I go through in a day and how sensitive I am to the smell of cakes?

Do they care?

Hands flap in the air, swatting me.

I guess that answers my question.

Reincarnation sucks.

TINY LULLABIES

Seaweed scratches my feet as I wade into the ripples of the moon. Behind me, the campfire burns. Waves drown out the strums of the guitar, the ex-boyfriend's never-ending lullaby.

"Over there," she shouts. "The rock."

I hoist myself up, switch on my flashlight.

Her necklace isn't there, only hundreds of tiny eyes on tiny shells, staring.

There's no time to scream. Their claws work fast.

Struggling to breathe, I reach out, skin dangling off the bone.

She kisses him, silhouetted in blazing orange, oblivious to tiny shells scurrying towards her.

I sink into a cacophony of screams and castanets.

MY SPACE

I remember playing with my busted-up Millennium Falcon and Mum saying my imagination could take me to the moon for real if I wanted it to.

I remember having that ambition too, before life's troubles got in the way.

I remember spiralling into a black hole and floating around, trying my best to disconnect myself from the world.

And I remember the exact moment when all that changed.

It was the day Eliza brought my son, Jacob, into the world.

I look around the flat, at the little space we have now, and I tell you, man, I'm up there.

THAT ONE GUY

"See?" Jim said. "Fridge magnets don't stick to themselves."

"Kind of like bestiality," Gordon said.

Everyone laughed apart from Jim. He shot Gordon daggers.

"Right. Cut that shit out. Some folks are trying to learn something, you know."

"Sorry, man," Gordon said, rolling his eyes, still smirking. "Just having a laugh."

"Aye? Well..." Jim scanned every face in the room. "As I was saying, fridge magnets don't stick to themselves." He glanced up, expecting another chuckle, another smart-arse comment. "You need to grip them tight, like this, or they'll leap right out of your hands."

"Just like bestiality," Gordon said.

PAPER PLANES

Paper planes were once a cry for help. Cutting myself wasn't. It was a means of escape.

As the curtains blew in, I breathed out and stepped onto the ledge. This time, ignoring the godless sky.

The crowd had more than doubled.

Brain-dead assholes below who'd never given me the time of day screamed internally: "Jump!"

I'd teased them already by slicing my finger with a pocketknife.

Pages torn from my journal, sticky with blood, were folded and ready for flight.

I watched them glide on the breeze.

Mouths snarled and snapped. Bodies clambered over each other for a taste.

tRAppEd

In my darkest time I was aware of everything. I was trapped, helpless, hearing strange muffled voices and laughter. No one heard me. I couldn't talk, let alone scream. All that kept me alive was a tube running into my stomach. Time was all I had.

Time to think.

Occasionally someone banged on the wall, asking if I was okay. God knows who they were. "You'll get out soon," they said.

I had to believe; had to trust someone.

It took forever. Then it happened. A tiny space.

Light burned my eyes. Screams, deafening screams, then: "Congratulations, it's a boy."

JUST A TOUCH

Late for school, Leah waited for the service bus.

Cold and hungry, she removed an apple from her bag.

It shrivelled in her hand before exploding to dust.

She breathed on her palms, easing the sting.

Her face tightened.

A black cat approached.

She bent and stroked him.

"Wow, mister cat," she said as his fur turned white. "It really is cold."

Finally, the bus arrived.

"Child, please," she said.

The driver smiled and handed her an OAP ticket.

Their fingers brushed.

She stared out of the window while the engine ticked over.

A red collar lay in the snow.

Not on the Right Track

When I was five, I spent every weekend on the train.

Mum had a new job. No one could look after me.

People asked, "Where's your parents?"

"Mum's being sick in the toilet," I'd say, which was true.

At least the men were nice, queueing up, making sure she was fine. But they'd be sweating buckets when they got out of that toilet with her.

I guess nobody enjoys seeing someone throw up.

Mum would come out wiping her mouth.

She got good money for that job.

Shame she had to spend it all on drugs to get through it.

SUNKEN YEARS

(POEM)

I'll meet you where the river runs dark, where it once shone gold, where ideas all sparked

I'll meet you by that fallen tree, where we scraped by thorns, watching daylight bleed

We'll walk along the rusty track, the railroad trail to the broken shack

And we'll talk until the sun goes down 'bout whatever makes the world go 'round

We'll spin into different times, hand in hand, connected minds

And we'll take that chance like we said we would, dance together and make things good

I will wait forever till the water clears to sail beyond those sunken years

DoWNHILL

When Chris found out about the cancer, it hit him pretty hard. So hard he disappeared for a month. When friends told me that he was trying to raise money, I had to see him.

"Why're you skateboarding again?" I asked him. "And bombing hills? You're gonna kill yourself, man."

"Does it matter?"

"Yeah, man. Fuck. Course it matters."

"Truth?" he said.

"Truth."

"If you're gonna go downhill then so am I."

"Look Chris, I'm fine, it's early stages."

"Maybe, but none of us know what lies ahead."

He smiled, adjusted his camera, then pushed off and rolled on down.

STARGAZING

Grandpa loved stargazing. He had eleven telescopes.

He'd talk about everything being magnified behind the lens.

I remember his shelves stacked high with big-ass books, his table covered in charts, notebooks, diagrams. Confusing-looking shit.

Me, I've got posters, videos, memorabilia, some good stuff. I thought I hit the jackpot when I got Milly. She's right here; gagged and tied to the bed. She don't look much like she does in them movies though, without makeup and all that ugly-crying.

Grandpa was right. Everything is magnified behind the lens.

I'm a stargazer just like him.

His obsession never twinkled out, though.

THE KICKER

Cameron used to annoy me by saying things like: "The eyes are the window to the soul," and: "days you don't laugh are days wasted." But yesterday, when Dave got in his face and yelled: "What fucking planet are you on, man?" I felt sorry for him.

Cameron composed himself, then slowly lifted his hand. "It's like a finger pointing to the moon," he said. "Don't concentrate on the finger or you'll miss all that heavenly glory."

Dave made an I-smell-shit face and said, "Who even talks like that?"

"Bruce Lee," Cameron said, then kicked him square in the balls.

LITTLE WHITE FLASHES

Severe storms were coming. Stay indoors they said.

The streetlights lit up at 4:30 p.m.

Darkness was creeping in.

He waited by the window, little white flashes catching his eye and he stared in awe, thinking about what was to come.

Another house stripped of its beauty; families left devastated.

His heart thundered. Adrenaline flooded his veins.

He gently opened the front door. She never heard a sound.

"Quiet," he whispered, wrapping his arm tight around her throat, undoing his belt with his other hand. "A storm is coming," he said.

Those little white flashes lay ripped on the floor.

FRED

Fred's in the pub writing down his phone number.

"You write sixes weird," Lisa says.

"Clockwise, yeah. Stir tea the same way. Writing anticlockwise is the Devil's work, you know, especially sixes."

"That's dumb."

"How?"

"Your name's Fred."

"So?"

"Well…" She holds up her phone, starts typing his name. "Look. Anticlockwise."

"Huh?"

Fred stands up, chucks his pint in Lisa's face, then storms out.

Later…

What if it's too late? he wonders, staring at his keyboard. *What if I'm the Devil? Fred… Fred…* over and over. "No!" he cries, pounding his fists against his skull. The room starts spinning anticlockwise.

DOING TIME

Twenty years it took for the cells to change my life.

I think back to my grandfather's sticky hands: simpler times when I didn't have to remind myself about putting things back.

Patrick, usually at the wind up, gave me good advice.

"Things get dirty inside," he said. "Stay focused. Adjustments take time. Solitude is part of the process."

I followed everything he said.

But now I'm old and forgetful and who needs a clocksmith these days anyway?

People use cell phones to tell the time.

So yeah, everything in this shop's for sale, apart from this: my grandfather clock.

oRgASMIC HEAVENLY BLISS

For Bryan, the empty bar was a far cry from good old party days and crazy wild sex. Alcoholic shakes were nothing but a distant memory.

Not that Bryan was a party goer, an alcoholic, or someone who'd ever had real sex.

No. Bryan was a mixologist: a professional cocktail maker who lived alone and loved his job. So much so that at night he'd shove his hands down his pyjamas, close his eyes and let his cocktail-shaking-fantasies fizz right into his subconscious: arm pounding away, creating orgasmic heavenly bliss.

Which funnily enough was the name of his first cocktail.

JUST TELL THE LADDIE

"No, he was literally spanking the monkey. He's banned from the zoo."

"Hahaha. Wasn't he thrown out of Tesco's for dancing with sausages or something?"

"It's not funny, but aye, bopping baloneys down the cold-meat aisle."

"Oaft. Ha-ha. Son or not, you're gonna have to explain masturbation properly to him."

"I'm trying. Can't have him choking any more chickens down at Fairline Farms."

"Hahaha."

"He's hitting Harvey's Bar later to play pocket pool. He's so bloody stupid; says he knows it's rough down there but promises he won't make the bald man cry or go boxing with that one-eyed champ."

After the Party

"He's still behind us."

"Just pull in, Danny."

"No, I'll go left."

"He's signalling."

"Damn it, I'm not pulling in. It's three in the morning."

"What's he want?"

"How the hell should I know, Cheryl? Shit. It's one way."

"Oh, God. What if something happens?"

"Stop panicking. You're not helping."

"Turn around."

"I can't, he's right behind me."

"What's that buzzing?"

"It's my phone. Answer it. It's in my jacket. Tell them someone's following us."

"Angela's calling. Who's Angela?"

"Just leave it, Cheryl..."

"I'll press loudspeaker."

"No. Don't."

"Danny! It's Angie. Colin knows about us. He's got a gun."

"Shit."

MARY S LETTER

"Mary's letters keep me going," Arthur says. "She never leaves without kissing my cheek."

"What're you searching for, Arthur?" the nurse says.

"Mary's letter. It's here somewhere."

The nurse hands him an old crumpled envelope. His eyes light up. His lips silently move as he reads.

"Look after that for me," he says, handing it back.

"Always do." The nurse pats her pocket.

"Huh? I don't understand. Is Mary not coming?"

"No, Arthur, she can't I'm afraid. Not today. But she told me to give you this."

She kisses his cheek, smiles, then winks to another nurse before walking away.

FIREWORKS

Fireworks through letterboxes had replaced knock-a-door-run in Glasgow. This was around 1984.

A local boy had gotten severely burnt. Mrs. Tabillo got the blame. It wasn't even her fault. The fireworks had been stolen from her shop.

Anyway, Henry was delivering her mail, and smelled gunpowder and urine through the letterbox. He saw her lying there and thought heart attack, fireworks. He reached inside the letterbox. The key, usually attached to some string, was gone. He ran to the phone box and dialled 999.

The police arrived, found a gun and a suicide note.

But that key was never found.

DAPHNE

"Push!" the doctor said.

Daphne was pushing, pushing with all her might, pushing so hard she thought her legs were about to fall off. She'd been warned of the dangers, that age might be a problem. But Daphne being Daphne was too stubborn to listen.

"That's it, Daphne," the doctor said. "Come on, you're doing great."

He was talking shit. She shouldn't have gone through with it, should have listened to her father.

"I don't care if it's a classic," her dad had said. "The car's £300. Even if it is a doctor selling it, it's gonna cause you problems."

PIPSQUEAKS

"Okay, team. Toilet break. Meeting resumes in five."

Eyes follow the MD as he leaves.

"What's that squeaking?" Jonathan asks.

"A mouse, probably. Place is falling apart."

"So, it's agreed, we need to get rid of him?"

"The mouse?"

"No, the old man."

"Ha. Yeah, we'll figure something out."

The door opens.

"Sorry about that," the MD says, sitting down. "Questions? Jonathan?"

"Yeah, what's that noise?"

The MD opens his drawer and smiles. "It's my old Dictaphone. Tape wheels are wearing out. Not complaining, though. It's outlasted two pacemakers. Just wanted to record today's meeting; sort out a few rats."

Boxing Clever

No point now saying that the high life of a prizefighter is short-lived, that you gotta make money fast and get out.

No point saying: don't get mixed up in the wrong kinda shit like betting on yourself and taking a fall for a pay-out that's larger than the match winnings.

Nope. No point. It's too far gone.

I didn't expect dirt to rain down on me like this, to be rocking and swaying on the ropes, taking slams to my sides, to my head.

I didn't expect to be boxed for real.

Boxed. Jesus Christ. Can anyone hear me?

THE CHAIR

Daddy was throwing away the old living-room chair. His eyes looked red and sore, a little like how mine felt, but then I'd been crying, and daddies never cry, do they? They're too big and strong.

"Doesn't it talk anymore?" I asked him. He looked puzzled. "The chair, you said it had a lot of stories to tell."

"Oh, yeah," he said.

"Does it know any about Mum?"

"Of course, darling, but we can make new ones."

"Promise?"

He didn't answer. Instead, he carried the chair back inside.

That day ended up being the most Daddy ever talked about Mum.

THE WRECK

It's a deep dive to the wreck. It's not the safest of waters either, but we're not worried. The sharks can't sense us.

We slip through the hole leading to the ship's centre: the Grand Hall, where food and wine was plentiful. The evenings were spent dancing to an orchestra, not one soul in the room knowing death was imminent.

The furniture crumbles with the slightest touch. Fish dart around trying to escape.

We glance at each other. It finally feels like closure.

Then the divers leave us.

I hold onto my daughter's hand as everyone, including us, fades away.

STAYING TRUE WITH TATTOOS

Sally booked herself into Mick's Tattoos for her eighteenth birthday, desperate for a Celtic band.

She was proud of her Scottish heritage but didn't tell anyone what she was getting. She said they would finally see who she really was and what she stood for.

"You'll feel a tiny scratch," Mick said.

"Yeah, everyone says that. Ow!" Sally whipped her arm away, leaving a three-inch black line.

"Damn it. I said don't move."

Mick tried again. Again, Sally pulled away, leaving another thin line.

It kept happening.

Sally eventually settled on a spider web.

She's been a goth ever since.

gUILTY PLEASURES

The stone-cold room reeked of death.

Her dad sat on the thick, wooden chair looking exhausted, surrounded by satisfactory looks of being caught and shamed.

Their eyes met, and he tried his best to keep it together, but he couldn't.

It came full force like lightning, and his eyes widened in tremendous panic. His body jolted. Clenching his teeth, he rose six inches.

There was a horrific squelching sound followed by the smell of burning meat.

With nothing left to give, he fell into a slump and everyone laughed.

The truth was out.

Her dad had been farting all along.

MONSTERS

Monsters under your bed? Nah, they can be anywhere. Most likely it's someone you know.

Mum and Dad never believed my nightmares, the things I'd see: children between ten and fourteen murdered. I was seventeen. I looked younger.

I knew where the monster would strike. If something didn't change soon, the nightmares would never stop.

Mum and Dad were on TV, crying and praying for my return. Watching it was upsetting, but it was too late.

I won't be around much longer.

The knife is pressed hard against my throat.

I tear it across quick, knowing children will be safe.

BALLOONED

With a headcount of fifty-three children and a handful of adults, his once easy-going balloon-modelling mantra of inflate, twist, inflate, twist, was about to burst.

Kids stuffed cake into their mouths, while dogs, giraffes, insects, and flowers became objects of desire for their young, grabby hands.

At the back of the room two children convulsed. They twisted and thrashed about as they clawed their throats. Their faces turned scarlet. Eyes puffed up and closed.

"Nut allergy!" a mother yelled.

"They're choking," cried another.

Inflate, twist, inflate, twist.

Words with a completely different meaning now.

Words he repeats in his sleep.

All Fired Up

"I might be eighty-two, but I'm not out of touch."

"Calm down, Gran."

"You young ones hang around that store. You don't talk to each other, head buried in your phones. You're drinking. You're smoking. You're all swearing."

"You just said we didn't talk."

"What about all that graffiti, then?"

"Eh? That's been there ten years."

"Well, it's new to me. And that fire?"

"What fire?"

"Last week. I saw smoke from my bedroom window. If I hadn't called the fire brigade that shop would've burnt to the ground."

"That was you?"

"Yep."

"But Gran, it was only someone vaping."

STICKS AND STONES

"Stephanie knows that tree gives me nightmares, Mummy."

"Don't be silly, Claire."

"It's not silly. Nobody believes me. She's always calling me scaredy-cat."

"Look, just remember the rhyme. *Sticks and stones may break my bones, names will never hurt me*."

"Names do, though."

"The rhyme, Claire. Okay?"

"Okay."

Stephanie was waiting by the wall. "Scaredy-cat, scaredy-cat!"

Not again, Claire thought. *Stick and stones, sticks and stones*.

The tree swayed, creaked and cracked as the branches stretched.

I knew it, I knew it Claire said to herself.

The branches burst through the wall grabbing Stephanie.

Sticks and stones. Sticks and stones.

BREWERS DROOP

Every weekend, same shit: Pete staggering down the street, cursing God, friendly one minute, boxing shirtless the next.

Nobody cared anymore. Curtains never twitched.

He dug around inside his pockets. "Shit!" He punched his front door. "Where's my fucking keys."

He kicked and roared until his throat was raw, until nothing came out but dry, painful whispers. And still, curtains never twitched.

Noticing his bedroom window open, he climbed the pipe.

He jumped to the ledge and pulled himself up.

The window slammed down on his fingers, leaving him wriggling around and screaming in silence.

Of course, curtains never twitched.

A WEE SEND OFF

The beach was the highlight of Grandpa's summer: building castles and burying each other in sand. But when Bruno came along, everything stopped. From that day forward Grandpa kicked that dog's arse. Not that Bruno stood for it. He chewed Grandpa's slippers even when they were still on his feet.

Years they battled.

Then, around Christmas, Grandpa passed away.

"Let's carry him outside before we call 999," Dad said. "Pack some snow over him, like old times."

We stood shivering, not noticing Bruno peeing everywhere.

"Look," Dad said. "It's a miracle. It's like sand."

Bruno grinned and took a shit.

THE BUS DRIVER

I accelerate, ploughing through large, steel gates that are no longer there, into a school that burned down several years ago.

My vision blurs: a mix of the state I was in before, and the state I'm in now, like underwater, drowning in fear. I can't be forgiven. Can't forgive myself.

Faces melt, eyes bulge and pop, bursting over small, charred bodies, sprawled across the hood of the bus.

Mothers shriek above the sound of crackling hair and skin.

A whiskey bottle clatters around the pedals.

Blackout.

Then I accelerate, ploughing through large, steel gates that are no longer there.

INTO THE BLACK

Garage locked and engine idling he sits, eyes closed, inside his shitty twelve-year-old Astra. A hosepipe runs from the exhaust to the rear window.

Tapping startles him.

Cable-tied to the steering wheel, he bucks and cries: "Help. Please."

Choking and sputtering, his face swells in the fog, eyes watery and wide.

She briefly removes her mask. "Breathe," she mouths, swirling her hands in an intake fashion. Then she replaces her mask, hiding the pain cooked up inside.

Blackness consumes the inside of the car, like his lungs, she imagines. Black as the shit her brother was injecting into his veins.

THE UNDERACHIEVER

"I was the underachiever: last in everything. I was either picked last or picked on. I was the geeky kid that everyone copied on tests: science, chemistry, you remember? I'd been flipping through those yearbooks. So many bad kids winning, making headlines. Not me. Not yet. So, how does this silver barrel feel against those gold teeth? Does blood taste like copper?"

"Mmmhmm."

"You forgot bronze is 88% copper, didn't you?"

"Hmmm?"

"Chemistry. Let me explain. Today feels like I've finally won all the medals. Bronze, silver and gold. Ha-ha! Get it? And this? Well, this here's my starting pistol."

THE LEVER

Naked, cold and shivering, I'm flat on my back staring at the chain around my feet, knowing this is all that's keeping me from getting out.

I've been in here so long my muscles have seized.

My wife is in the next room.

There's no mistaking those moans, those screams.

She's next.

I can do this.

I stretch my calf, toes barely reaching the lever.

Pipes rattle through the walls.

"Don't you dare!" she yells.

What have I done? I could have made this last longer.

"Hurry up," she says. "The kids need a bath tonight as well you know."

THE ISLAND

"Seven years alone. You can't imagine it. When the sea wasn't an angry whisper, it was a worn-out blue heartache. Every "Can I do this?" and "Fuck you!" to the sky was a cry for help. God knows I must've rebuilt that raft a hundred times. So much fear. So much uncertainty."

"But you survived." *The phone-speaker crackles.* "Remember... I was alone, too."

"Sorry."

"It's okay."

"So, did the insurance pay out?"

"Nah, you never signed the documents."

"What? So, the whole hide-on-a-fucking-island plan was a waste of time?"

"Yeah... and... um... I got kinda bored waiting... So, I remarried."

cLASSIcS

"Okay class, beginning Monday, we'll be reading Orwell's Animal Farm. Go home. Practice. Gain some confidence over the weekend."

Monday.

"That was a very mature and impressive reading, Jimmy."

"Thanks. Dad helped."

"Fantastic."

"Yeah, we talked, watched movies. One was about a boy. Well, not a real boy. He was telling lies. But his father loved him. Pin... Pino or something. There was a tiny man, too. Insect? Pino? Can't remember.

"Pinocchio?"

"Maybe."

Home.

"Told you, Son."

"Teacher said to bring that movie in."

"Really? Who'd have thought it. Animal Farm at school, and now incest porn. School sounds great."

BAKER'S DOZEN

3 am. Clock's set. Heat's turned up.

Jeff says he'll concentrate on the dough, the easy part.

Nigel's talking about combinations, sounding flustered.

"Keep it simple, guys. Keep it sweet. Don't want things getting nutty."

"Gotcha, Chef."

Twelve headstrong dudes, all throwing ideas into the mix.

"Do your own bit. Concentrate on nothing but the load."

"Gotcha, Chef."

My name's Baker. Funny, huh? Even funnier, I can't cook worth a damn. Love the terminologies though. Think Ocean's Twelve: that shitty cash-in Clooney movie. That's us, without the shitty cash-in of course. We're set for life.

"Three minutes, guys."

"Gotcha, Chef!"

Remembered

Silent Night pulls me out of the gunfire and blood-curdling screams.

On your feet, soldier!

I bang the heel of my hand against the frozen window frame, cracking it open. There's a rusty-red Volvo on a blanketed street, a bandaged wound, footprints, hundreds of them.

The sky ignites in green and white.

Get down soldier!

Photographs topple and smash. I reach for my wife, crumpling her to my chest.

Quiet. Shadows. Whispers.

"Leave it there for him," someone says.

Everything quietens.

I unlock the door.

A box flaps open in the breeze. Tins. Food.

In the distance, a choir sings.

CHINESE INSTRUCTIONS

Ken phoned "The Long Wok" at 6pm on Christmas Eve. He wasn't hungry. He needed help building Joshua's presents he'd bought on eBay. The instructions were all in Chinese.

He ordered noodle soup. *I'll make it worth their while*, he thought.

"So busy," Shen said. "Time of year, crazy."

Ken seized his moment. "I could deliver those if you wouldn't mind building my toys?"

Relieved, Shen agreed. An hour later, Ken returned.

"Deliver okay?" Shen asked.

"Yeah, folks weren't happy, though."

"How? Food no good?"

"No, they didn't expect me at the door. They bought the same toys off eBay."

TURN UP FOR CHARLIE

Bad feelings spiralled inside long before Derek summoned me into the office.

Last week, he threatened to sack Charlie if he couldn't operate the cable-winder. Thing was, I should've been watching over him.

Charlie had gotten himself into a panic: started sweating, had the place reeking of rotten turnips. So, I got him some deodorant. There's a juddering slam. Charlie's tie had caught around the reel, mashed his face to pulp.

Think that's crazy? That's nothing. I'm stomping on Derek's head like a maniac. Air smells sweet as roses. Well, in my mind, because actually it reeks of rotten turnip.

FEELING YOUNG AGAIN

She gave me the eye. I didn't know what to make of it. Then she stood over me, loosening the straps.

"Put one in each hand," she said. "Use your thumbs." I couldn't stop grinning. A laugh escaped. An old man, handling things like these? Wow. "Don't worry," she said. "You'll be fine. You'll find your rhythm."

"My goodness," I said. Then she put this mask over my eyes.

"Don't move." I couldn't. I was terrified. "Let me turn you on."

I took a breath.

PlayStation flashed across the screen.

Beat Saber.

I didn't know what the fuck was happening.

THE BUNDLE OF BLANKETS

Kami heard the baby's cry and ran to what she first thought was a bundle of blankets outside the church.

"Don't like God either, huh?" she said, lifting him, making light of an ugly situation, even though it was her truth.

Last weekend she'd split with Michael. "Horror movies are despicable, sinful," he'd said. "Choose... Your collection or me?"

She finger-brushed the baby's fine hair, revealing three comma-shaped curls.

A birthmark?

She gasped, throwing him to the ground.

"No!" Michael cried, running from the shadows. "My sister's baby." He dropped to his knees. "I... I just wanted you back, Kami."

WEIGHTLESS

I was weightless in the blinding light, life flashing before my eyes.

Forget 8K and 7.1 channel sound. I relived infancy right into adulthood in seconds. That's right. All of the emotions.

Creatures with grey, toad-like skin chattered in whispers, contented bees in a hive. Old people with missing limbs inside clear sacks, creaked and swung above, faces fixed in screams.

My every right and wrong suddenly burst my heart. More pain than pleasure.

Oval-shaped heads tilted like confused puppies: huge, black, inquisitive eyes.

Nightmare-inducing dentistry tools lay beside me.

What if these old people arrived here young like me?

TOY BOY

Twins, Janet and Leanne, are discussing the single life.

"Let's find someone younger," Leanne says.

"Seriously?" Janet smiles at the thought.

"Why not?" Leanne searches her phone. "Here's one."

Looking for a toy boy? Wanna ride all night?

Andrew: Eighteen, seeks two women, thirty-plus.

Janet gasps. "That's just wrong."

"How?"

"We're forty-two."

They both laugh but decide to meet up with him.

"Twins," Andrew says, pointing his fingers like pistols. "Bullseye!"

Cute, Janet thinks.

The following week at the hotel...

Andrew opens the bathroom door dressed as Woody from Toy Story. He throws them a horse costume.

"Bullseye!" he says.

THE BooK RESToRER

Restoring books for twenty years, Carlton saw his wife much like he saw his work: damaged, delicate and unhinged.

She needed medical therapy. His therapy lay under a magnifying glass.

They were oddly matched, living separate lives until Cynthia began decluttering the house: Blu-rays and DVDs going first.

"We have Netflix," she said. "You have a Kindle. Books are going."

She got in his face.

"Enough," he said.

He shoved her.

She tumbled down the old stairs, battering the edges. She landed crumpled in the dust: jacket torn, spine snapped.

Again, he saw her much like he saw his work.

THE TWILIGHT SAGA

Larry loved Edward from Twilight. He dressed like him, talked like him and even had that lustful, smoky-eye thing going on. If he could be sparkly then his look would be complete. He grabbed his old laptop and fired up Google.

An ad for a limited-edition Twilight-Sparkle costume appeared, but the image kept failing to load.

He cursed his shitty laptop, but those five-star ratings pushed his excitement through the roof. The one-size-fits-all costume was only £14.99.

Three weeks later a tiny box arrived. Inside was an even tinier costume.

The package read: Compatible with My Little Pony Twilight Sparkle.

MISTLETOE AND WINE

The Christmas cards are ripped up, the tree's down: decorations, the lot. Would've said forget it if the grandkids weren't still coming over.

I imagined endless questions.

Where's Granny? She coming home? Have you been crying?

Yesterday I tried on my Santa suit. When the jacket wouldn't fasten, I broke down. Jeanie, my wife, was drunk, couldn't stop laughing. She phoned our daughter and told the grandkids Santa wasn't real.

She's not laughing anymore, though. She's wearing that Santa outfit and spewing up outside: diced carrots everywhere.

But what am I going to say now? The reindeer had dodgy guts?

THE ARMY TANK

"Can Sid stay, Mum?"

"Sure. Feel sorry for that boy. People say he's a bad egg. I blame his parents."

"Me too. They've still not fixed those stairs he keeps falling down."

Mum sighed.

Christmas was six weeks away. Sid said he'd found his presents, could help me find mine if I wanted. I didn't tell him that Mum said Santa would know if I went snooping.

Anyway, we found Action-man figures, aeroplanes, even a tank.

But when Christmas came the tank wasn't there.

Mum was right. Santa must've known.

At least Sid got one, though. Shame it looked second-hand.

SNIPPETS AND RIPPLES

(POEM)

Books stop minds from committing crimes. Genius.

His sentence was shortened. All the while his thoughts remained twisted.

He was out by the rocks. Kids bombed up and down the river, drunk out of their minds: drugs most likely, probably lines.

If his head weren't buried inside a book, no question he'd be back inside.

He looked up as someone fell in.

Fun, he thought, as the boat spun

It wasn't shrieks of joy anymore.

"The propeller!" someone cried.

He laughed watching it chop and grind.

Snippets and ripples. Poetry by the beach.

Finally, a title.

He wrote between screams.

POSSESSION

"Mum, come quick, something's not right.

"I can't. I'm busy just now."

"No, you're not listening. She's just staring… and making weird noises. She's not the same, Mum. I'm telling you she's not the same."

"For goodness sake Abigail, you're hysterical. What the hell's so bad? Can't it wait?"

"No. Her head's spinning around. She's trying to kill me. I'm not lying."

Mum rushes to the room, opens the door to what looks like the aftermath of a pillow fight, feathers everywhere, shit running down the walls.

"Jesus Christ. Right, that's it. Tomorrow I'm getting rid of that bloody owl."

LOVELY PINS

Pleasantries at work are difficult enough, never mind with someone opposite you who's dating your ex-boyfriend and asking about his likes and dislikes. He's a shitbag, but so is she, for stealing him.

She talks about having kids somewhere down the line.

I humour her.

They've dated a month. He hates kids.

All he cares about are those long legs. Lovely pins, as he once said to me.

I spy condoms in her bag and unclip a safety pin.

Lovely pins, I remind myself, lovely pins.

Three condoms in a packet.

I smile, poking this lovely pin through each one.

GRANDMA'S HOUSE

It's horrible to say Mandy's Grandma's passing was good timing, but we couldn't stay with my mum any longer.

"Maybe it's haunted here," I said, opening another tin of paint.

Mandy went quiet.

Later, in bed, I asked: "How long's this gonna last?"

Silence.

"Fine. Be like that." I turned over.

"Michael," she whispered. "My family refused this house."

"Why?"

"They felt… unsafe."

I went mental. "It's not fucking haunted, Mandy!" I threw back the covers, grabbed my clothes, quickly got dressed, then stormed out, slammed the door.

The walls shook.

It's horrible to say, but it was good timing.

PUSHERS

"Back then, pushers were on every street corner. Shit's goddamn changed and not for the better. It's all about the money and who's got the best ride. I see them pass my window, five miles per hour and shit. I know what they're trying to do. Trying to make a fool out of an old man, that's what it is."

"But Grandpa."

"Grandpa nothing. You're just on their side anyhow, flashing those goddamn rings around."

"But it's… it's... You'd rather it was like before?"

"Damn right. Hands are meant for pushing, not flicking some doohickey on a stupid-ass electric wheelchair."

oAT FLAKES

She'd been awake since 4 a.m. because of my itching.

After we changed the bed, she said she'd grab another hour. I went downstairs, searched YouTube and found this guy talking about sprinkling oat flakes into a warm bath. He had before-and-after shots. It looked ideal.

Oh well, goodbye breakfast.

I'm soaking away when the wife comes in. We've got a "No can do, if it's a number two" rule, but she takes a look in the bath. Big mistake.

Before I can explain, she's yelling: 'Ralph and Huey' down the long, white telephone.

It's goodbye breakfast for her, too.

BURgER joInT

McDonald's smells amazing, but everyone's staring at me, and I hate that shit, so I check out the rad spaceship and alien toys in the cabinet.

Someone taps my shoulder.

"Are you forty-seven?" a bearded guy asks. He's carrying books.

Cheeky bastard, I'm thirty-two. I shake my head, thinking, *idiot.*

"Fifty-five," the cashier says.

I realise I'm holding a ticket, number forty-seven. What a fuckwit. I chuckle to myself, grab my bag of cold burgers and plod home.

"Interview go okay?" Dad asks.

"Interview?"

"The job… McDonald's?"

"Um… they said they'd call."

I knew I shouldn't have had that spliff.

TOTAL STONER

Arnold spent his holiday drunk and stoned as usual, thinking about his job, thinking about writing.

"Cannabusiness survive after an alcoholiday?" he said and laughed. Franco, his basset hound, stared vacantly, eyes like tomatoes wrapped in cellophane. "You hungry pal?" Arnold asked. "I've got pies... Hey, if you eat pie lots, aeroplanes won't leave the ground. Pilots, get it?" Franco huffed, Arnold kept smoking and giggling and writing in his notebook. Eventually, he passed out.

Franco got the munchies, snatched the notebook off the table.

One gulp. Gone.

"Dognabbit!" Arnold said, "That's it. This idea's buried. I'm fetching a beer."

KILLER INSTINCT

Hunched down beside an old picket fence, hidden in the shadows, he watches them go about their business.

The sensor light comes on, startling him. A young girl looks out the window. Luckily, the sensor goes off again before she sees him.

He'd avoided this town, knew it wasn't safe. Too many people around.

Where has he gone? his family wonders. Why is he taking so long?

When he returns, they're curious about the blood.

He doesn't care. He will clean later. For now, he remains silent and proud as he drops the rabbit, sliding it over with his nose.

HEADING FOR THE LIGHT

Gloria stumbled around in the blizzard. Everything, bar a single streetlight, blurred into one.

Not a soul around. No traffic. Nothing.

Approaching the light, she realised there was a car on its side.

She wiped the windshield. A man, unconscious, head split to his nose, hung over his seatbelt.

"Come on!" she yelled, tugging the door. "Come. On!"

It must be frozen. Maybe it's locked.

She rocked the car.

Too much weight. Too much…

The car fell with her, but it wasn't her life that flashed by.

It was curiosity.

Why does that bag in the back seat look familiar?

BURNOUTS

Tires squeal outside.

"Bastardin' burnouts," he says, closing the blinds.

He shuffles into the kitchen, pours another whiskey.

"Getting too much around here, Annie," he says to the empty room.

The candle is still burning away on the tiny cake. He wipes his eyes, raises his glass again. "Happy birthday, Annie," he says.

His grandson was here last time, laughing and joking. This was before he was racing with those nutters outside, before Annie was knocked down.

He sits and sips, thinking about life as the candle burns out, wondering why his grandson never calls.

Hope I'm wrong, he thinks.

A BIT OF A WRESTLING MATCH

"What're the seagulls doing, Granddad?"

"It's a rain dance, Son. They're getting worms."

"Oh, I thought they needed the toilet."

"Heheheh. Right enough. You dance like that waiting on Grandma. She takes forever pulling them tights up, eh?"

"Is Grandma a superhero?"

"What?"

"A superhero. They wear tights."

"Nah, Grandma's a wrestler."

"Really?"

"Christ, Jimmy. Get a grip, son. You've got high school after summer. Toughen up."

"Maybe I could learn to wrestle."

"Give me strength… Go bother Grandma. I'm needing to pick my bunions."

"Okay."

Later…

"Granddad?"

"What now?"

"Is Grandma's face meant to go blue in a headlock?"

TRIED AND DENIED

"What is this spooning business anyhow?"

"It's what the young ones do, Jack," Betty said.

"I'm eighty-three. You're seventy-eight. Forget it."

"But don't you wish we were young again?" she said. Jack went quiet. "Remember our wedding?"

Jack smiled. "That I do," he said.

"Well?"

"Aye, okay then." Jack turned over.

Betty brought herself closer. "Jeez, your arse is like ice," she said.

"I can't help it. It's my tablets."

"The tablets make your arse cold?"

"Aye, and my front bits, too. I don't even know where my wee thing is half the time."

Betty turned back over. "Goodnight, Jack."

BROKEN LEGS

"I tripped over in the street."

"If you don't mind me saying, Mr. Ambers, you're not exactly a big guy, are you? So, God knows how you managed to break both legs. Are you sure that's all that happened?"

"Are you calling me a liar?"

"Not at all. But surely you can see where I'm coming from."

"I can't see anything."

"Hmm, okay, we'll fix you up and we'll take it from there. Have a seat, Mr. Ambers." Ernie sits down. "My goodness these are at funny angles, aren't they? You tried superglue?"

"Superglue? Christ! Just give me new glasses!"

I HAVE THE POWER

Mum bought my first guitar thirty years ago. She said I was too old for He-Man toys. She's in the audience tonight and I can't stop biting my nails.

As if mocking me, the guy on stage plays fingerstyle.

I throw away my only pick and head backstage to down some whiskey.

I start kicking the wall.

CRACK!

My boot's off. My toe's huge. The nail's hanging.

"Fucking perfect!"

"Five minutes, Mr. Vassallo," a voice says.

I take another swig before hobbling on, expecting fabulous secret powers to be revealed to me as I hold aloft my crusty-cheese guitar pick.

TIME TO DO THE RIGHT THING

Five years is a flicker on the outside.

Inside, it's a lifetime.

Prison's made my hair white. Not through worry, though. Through guilt.

They were good people I took from. Made an honest living. I was down, living rough, starving. I remember shaking like I'd come in from the cold. Their little girl startled me. My damn gun went off.

Murphy talks too much in his sleep: little girls, boys. Horrible things.

I covered his face with a pillow to shut him up.

He's quiet now. He ain't waking up.

But I have.

Plenty folks here need fixing.

Me too.

THE FEAR OF DROWNING

Daddy wouldn't buy me ice cream.

I heard him say to Mom: "Pa threw me in the river when I was eight, said I'd better learn fast. Well, I wasn't hanging around to be rescued. All I'm saying is, let her get on with it. Let her kick and thrash all she wants. She'll work it out. Look, she's tensing up and holding her breath now."

No wonder. I was terrified.

All the way home from the beach, I sat quiet.

"We didn't even have to do anything," Mom said.

"I know," Daddy said. "It's weird. Her tantrums just stopped."

INSoMNIA

One o'clock, two o'clock, three o'clock. Stop! I wish it would. Brain's flying all over the place. How many hours is it before you hallucinate? Seventy-two? Must be hitting that now. I'm seeing some freaky shit in the shadows, man, I tell you, voices too. Every morning, and I can't stop pacing up and down, worrying about everything and nothing all at once. Sort it out, Sam, I tell myself. Think, man, think. Okay… watch the clock.

9:22 a.m.

Voices outside.

Yes.

 "You hear about Sam?" a woman says. "Tragic, it was. Poor lad died in his sleep, Monday night."

THE BISCUIT FACTORY

First day at Dumble's Biscuit Factory and I wasn't even in the job five minutes before Archie asked me to get "the long stand" from the storeroom.

I was twenty-five, not some naïve apprentice who was about to get caught out with that one. But not to disappoint, I honoured his request, returning two hours later, face a fiery red.

The guys were doubled up, pissing themselves laughing.

"Did you get your long stand?" Archie asked, thinking he got me good.

"No," I said. "I've been outside, had a cup of tea and a cigarette. It's bloody scorching out there.

THE MONEY LENDER

"The Mets game is in the bag," Curtis said. "Our team's on fire."

When they lost, however, poor Curtis was set alight and distinguished with baseball bats.

Silas loved making things personal if you didn't pay up.

Same thing happened to Henry Tarlano, a good friend of mine, who borrowed money for his operation but couldn't afford the interest. A month before he was due in, he was hospitalised.

Now I'm speeding along on choppy waves and Silas is tied up.

"Loan shark, right?" I say to him. "I know you like to make things personal. Guess where you're going."

LOST IN THE MALL

Lucas had gotten lost in the shopping centre again.

"Come on," she said. "You know Mummy's sorry, right?"

He looked up, eyes brimming with tears, bottom lip quivering. "Silly sausage," she said, tousling his hair.

The corners of his mouth turned up, then he dragged his sleeve across his nose. "I want Daddy," he said, his voice hitching.

"Daddy's in the car waiting, okay?"

"Promise?"

"Promise. Now stop snivelling. People are looking."

He sighed then took her hand.

Soon they were marching through the car park, her grip tightening. "Ow," he yelped. "Where's Daddy's car?" She never answered. "Where's Mummy?"

MISTY DAYS

"I can't see our house," Alice said, clutching her mother's hand.

"It's there, Honey. Don't worry."

During thunderstorms Alice hid under her blankets. She'd jam her fingers in her ears, wishing time would pass quickly. It never did.

The mist is kinda like a blanket, Alice thought.

"We'll be home soon," Mum said as the mist grew thicker. Only their clasped hands were visible. "It's not so bad."

"Yeah," Alice said, thinking her mother's voice sounded croaky.

Gaining confidence, Alice's grip loosened. Her mother's hand somehow seemed fragile, featherlike.

As the mist cleared, their eyes met.

Alice got her wish.

BoRRoWiNg

Gary calls it borrowing but never gives anything back, even on a small scale, like the tools he borrowed from me that lie at the bottom of his skip, underneath old doors, bricks and glass.

Yeah, he thinks he's the bigger man, thinks waving a Mossberg Shotgun in folks faces stops them asking questions.

We're supposed to be friends, partners. He hides the evidence, plans escape routes, and takes seventy percent.

As he chucks the bag into the car, the alarm bells ring.

Well, they don't for him.

I slam the accelerator, laughing as he shrinks in the rear-view mirror.

THE BIG RIDE

Ella had one thing on her mind as the Big Wheel reached the top, and no thick, grey clouds were going to stand in her way.

"What if it rains?" Patrick asked.

"Shush," she said. "As long as it's not cold we'll be fine." She glanced at his crotch and winked.

He sighed. The sky rumbled.

"Ignore it," she said, straddling him.

The sky flashed twice.

"Christ, we might get electrocuted."

"Quiet."

"Someone might see us."

"For goodness sake, Patrick."

When the Big Wheel stopped, Patrick heard laughter from the kiosk. The sign above read: collect your souvenir photos here.

RocKStaR STATUS

"Why the new album after eight years, Carl?" A reporter asked.

Carl grinned. "The truth? Girls, man. Always the girls, right?"

He flared his nostrils, patted his flabby gut and scanned the room with his beady eyes.

Laughter erupted.

"Hey, there's just more of me to love now, right?" he added.

"And girls want that?"

"Always."

"That make you happy?"

"For a minute or two, yeah."

"You're saying you only last a minute or two?"

More laughter.

"No, I'm saying women are okay for a minute or two."

Silence.

Bedtime...

He unscrewed the hand-cream jar and reached for the tissues.

GOING DOWN?

Unlike Harry, chasing girls wasn't my thing. But last month something snapped, literally.

I took a sneaky photo of this blonde girl on the train.

Later, she was on the second floor of the mall. I jumped in the elevator, banged on the glass to get her attention. Next thing, lift's plummeting.

Doctor says I'm lucky it's only amnesia. Harry thinks it's hilarious, digs the photo of her though.

But here, the news this morning, that girl: raped and murdered.

I'm worried sick. Can't remember one day from the next.

What if? Oh, God.

What if it's true about Harry?

MARMALADE MAID

Emptiness was everywhere: the cracked vase in the bedroom, her husband's eyes, her heart.

"Need more marmalade, Barbara!" he yelled.

"Get it yourself, Eric. I'm in the bath!"

"So?"

Barbara eventually got out. Eric was flat on his back, staring at the ceiling, empty jar by his side, spoon lodged in his throat.

She studied his eyes.

The light was gone, but at least from this angle he was looking at her.

Warmth filled her heart.

She wondered if the marmalade jar would make a good replacement for the vase.

She dislodged the spoon and lifted his eyelid.

Then scooped.

WORLDWIDE LOTTERY

Let me tell you a secret. Him and I have a little lottery going on. Yes, Him. The Big Guy upstairs.

The numbers come out but we can never decide what street to choose, what country to pick from. It's all light-hearted fun, really. He has his reasons. As do I. Reasons you'll never know or figure out. One week it's my turn, next week it's his.

You see: everyone is bad, everyone is good.

You know that because you're not so perfect.

I just wanted to let you to know that your door number has come up many times.

Box of Pampers

Laura doesn't think.

"That's one big dirty bum," she said, unwrapping the Pampers, oblivious to the homeless guy walking past.

I tried explaining. His fists were already up. He started shoe shuffling and everything, getting right into it, unaware a shit-filled nappy was under his feet.

Then he slides a beauty.

Later I suggested to Laura we should make it up to him, buy a voucher for the spa or something, make him king for a day.

"What's this?" he said, opening the envelope. "Enjoy your day of pampering? Pampers is it?"

He raised his fists and began shuffling again.

cRicKET MATCH

She screamed.

"Do that again, and I'll bat your husband's head off." He towered over her. She bit her lip. "This is happening," he said. "Understand?"

She nodded.

"Wh-what do you want?" her husband stammered.

"You both want to live?"

They nodded, a begging nod. Then he tapped the cricket bat on each of their shoulders. "Oh, that's real love right there, isn't it?" he said.

The couple shared a glance.

"No," he said. "Hold that gaze."

They did.

He watched their chests heave and their tears flow.

"Question. Why did each of you pay me to kill the other?"

Rugby Match

An unsettling impatience brewed during the six nations Scotland v England match at Murrayfield Stadium.

Things aren't looking friendly out there, Stevie thought. Someone is going to get hurt.

People were all shouting different things at once. Stevie couldn't concentrate, wondered if he should get out now.

Bodies pushed and shoved. Faces got battered and squashed. The ground became more and more slippery. He kept glancing up at the clock.

"I'll be glad when this is over," he said. "I can't even see the bloody game from here."

He wiped his brow, closed the till and took the next order.

THE BONFIRE

"Alia lost her arm in the fire."

"What?" Mum said. "When?"

"At the bonfire yesterday."

"Jesus Christ, is she okay?"

"Brad said she was howling down the street."

"My God, where was her mum and dad?"

"They weren't watching."

"That's terrible. The poor wee thing. I… I can't believe it. Is she in hospital?"

"They don't have hospitals for dolls, Mum."

"Dolls? Eh?"

"It was her doll's arm."

"Jeez, Raymond. You need to be careful how you say things."

"Sorry. Her dress caught fire, too"

"She'll get another one for her dolly."

"No. Alia's dress caught fire."

"Oh, for fu…"

WRITING ADVICE

Writing advice? Don't bloody listen to it.

The wife called, questioning my whereabouts. My wages weren't reflecting the time I was out of the house.

Find a quiet place, they said.

When I returned, the air was sour with alcohol and vomit. She was sprawled on the chair, my diary in her hand, opened at the page where I'm sleeping with another woman.

Write about what you know, they said. Exaggerate the truth, they said.

I shook her. Pills flew off her t-shirt. I yelled "Wake up!" But she was limp, wasn't listening.

I shouldn't have listened.

Bloody writing advice.

THE RENT

"Aren't we square?" I ask deliberately looking vague.

"Think he's forgetful, Tommy," Ali says, tapping his head.

"Heard our wives joking about the old grey matter of his yesterday."

Cool.

Carol walks in. "What's up, Tommy?"

"He's saying the rent's square. Ali reckons it's that old grey matter of his. He heard you and his wife talking."

Carol side-eyes me. "Um, you're not angry, Tommy?"

"Not if he's genuine."

"Really? Okay, it's true. That mattress is disgusting. My hands and knees get filthy, and…"

"Wait, what? Filthy? Mattress?"

"Grey mattress. What you said."

"Grey. Matter!"

Tommy glares at me.

Shit.

LOOSE CHANGE

You'd see her wandering the streets. She looked mid-forties, kinda hard to tell with her weather-beaten skin. She was pleasant enough, unlike some of the homeless around here who wouldn't think twice about stabbing you.

It was Saturday afternoon. She looked like she was raging about something. Her face was beetroot.

Some old, heavy-bearded guy was storming away from her, mumbling. "She's bloody menopausal," he said as he passed.

I walked over. She was counting her coins. "You alright?" I asked.

"Just going through the change," she said.

"Funny, that old guy just said that."

She started screaming at me.

HOOKED

Max's addiction became clear when his weight plummeted. Watching his whole world fall apart made me smile.

He was trying in vain for a fix and no one cared.

We were all in the same boat, out for ourselves.

Max was raging, completely out of line.

He stared at me, itching, but I ignored him.

I watched with bated breath as he approached.

He threw one of his best hooks, expecting me to take it.

I got up.

 "You're not bribing me with that," I said. "You're getting nothing from me. Face it, Max, the fishing contest's over. You're done."

SHAKE IT OFF

Gerry, our Border Collie, is a shaker. Not the I'm-terrified-of-everything kind, but the kind who shakes dry after a spit of rain. He loves rolling in mud, too. I'm fine with that now.

He found his way next door.

If my neighbour wasn't such an arsehole with his pigeons I might've have done the neighbourly thing and blocked the hole, but I was sick of hosing bird shit off my path.

"Ben!" his wife shouted. "What're you feeding those birds? The bedsheets are all splattered."

I finished hosing Gerry down and I swear he was actually smiling.

Pals for life.

BUTTER KNIFE

"Jenna!"

"It's a butter knife, Daddy. I can't kill myself."

"Well…" He looks out the window. "Wait, is that an ambulance outside Mrs. Fallon's?"

"Yeah."

"Oh, dear."

"What?"

"Probably gone to the big one in the sky."

"Like Jack and the Beanstalk?"

"No," Daddy laughed. I mean… Up there."

"With Bailey?"

"Mmhmm."

"Wish I was."

Daddy knelt, turned Jenna to face him. "Don't wish that."

"But I thought dying didn't hurt?"

"Not for your dog, and maybe when you're old, but... it's… complicated."

Later…

 "You still playing Minecraft on my Kindle?"

"No, I'm asking Alexa if a butter knife hurts."

SAVE THE CHILDREN

"Grab the railing!" he yelled to the boys. "I'll save you. I'll save you all!"

Trembling and wide-eyed, the boys held tight.

How much longer could he paddle? Splinters sank into the creases of his hardened palms. Veins swelled in his forearms. Spray came up from the paddle and almost blinded him. Blood, so much blood.

Don't count the rows, he reminded himself. *Whatever it takes. Whatever it takes.*

"Why is this happening to us, Father?" Tears spilled down the boy's cheeks.

"Don't worry. You're next."

"But I'm scared."

Father paddled harder. Paddled until it broke like the boy's coccyx.

BIRTHDAY BEERS

Craig was heading home with a bag full of beers in the blazing sun. The party was later. A swim was in order.

An hour passed.

"You forget something?" a guy shouted, waving a phone.

"Holy shit. Thanks, man. I owe you. What's your name?"

"Farley."

"Well, Farley…" Craig eyed the beers by his clothes. "Help yourself."

"Really?"

"Sure, just don't leave me dry, okay?"

"Gotcha man, thanks."

Craig hit the showers.

Farley took the clothes, the towels and left the beers, wondering why someone would want to walk home soaking wet. Then he stepped outside into the blazing sun.

BIRTHDAYS

"Whatcha thinkin' 'bout Trevor?"

"The zoo… last year's birthday, when I was ten. Thinking about school as well. I used to hate that place. Missing it now, though. Mum and Dad hated their jobs, you know. Said they felt trapped. Not trapped like my granny who's up in that care home. She tried leaving with us last time we visited. Care homes are like jail, aren't they? Is everybody just a prisoner? Am I?"

"No Trevor. This is where you get well. And you're not eleven today, I'm afraid. You're forty-three."

"Oh." Trevor quietens.

"Whatcha thinkin' 'bout Trevor?"

"The zoo…"

HIM

(POEM)

Him who was inside of me. Him when I screamed no.

Him that only wanted me Saturday nights while drunk. Him that flung fists when I told him to go.

It was him who left me. Him who lived with her.

Him who hid between his job and friends with that cockiness and happy demeanour.

It was him they all trusted. Him they loved.

Him with no worries. Him with the golden touch.

Him that made me have this abortion. Him that drunk his last.

Him who never noticed the powder around the rim of the glass.

Him no more.

cUTTINg-EDgE ARt

She wanted to paint my portrait.

Being her carer, I was flattered. She'd been on suicide watch for two months and we hadn't quite bonded yet. Sharp objects were a no go. Even the paintbrushes had rounded ends. She kept glancing over the top of the easel with those intense green eyes, replacing sheet after sheet, becoming increasingly frustrated. Her desire for perfection was difficult to endure.

"It doesn't have to be brilliant," I said.

She collapsed. Her arm flopped into view, covered in thin, tiny cuts. The used sheets of paper lay scattered around her, each with red edges.

EIRA

Eira practiced holding her breath so that she didn't get another mouthful of toilet water like the last time.

Every night she'd fill her bath to the top.

"What're you up to in there?" Her mother asked.

About three minutes now, Eira thought.

Walking home, Eira saw one of the bullies chasing another girl, chasing her right across the frozen lake. She heard cracks. Soon they were thrashing and screaming in the icy water.

Eira took a deep breath, knowing it was the right thing to do.

Two girls were saved that day.

Only two.

Eira and her new friend.

FINAL DRIVE

It was a hell of a drive and I was doing my best not to think about killing the guy I'd taken on board. There was still a fair way to go and no matter how I looked at it, he was in my line of sight every few hundred yards, in my ear, and it was constantly chipping away. I'd had enough.

I've hit plenty of rough spots in the past, of course. None like this. A little slice here and there. I just lost it.

Whatever you say, it takes balls, man.

And my caddy forgot them, too.

ZoMBiE

It was a question we'd asked each other as kids: what would you do if you were faced with a zombie?

Kick him in the nuts and run, I'd say. And we'd laugh.

George, being practical, said he'd chop off his head with an axe. When that day came, I froze. My heart pounded so hard I could hear it.

Nowadays, I struggle to picture life before the outbreak; struggle to visualise anything.

Sometimes the old mind returns, and I wonder if George is still around. Mostly, I just keep shuffling along: hungry, listening; never hearing, never feeling, my heart.

fREEdoM

Tourists in Scotland? Bring them in. I'm even wearing my kilt right now. So what if they think it's like Braveheart and Rob Roy and we're all living in the Highlands chasing sheep?

I'll shout "Freedom!"

I'll crack a wee smile.

I'm not that same grumpy old bastard who moaned about Christmas or complained about the beach. Not anymore. That's all in the past. It was the sand, the pine needles, getting stuck inside the old underpants, see.

Well, I don't really mean see. I've still got scars after clawing myself stupid. But aye: tourists, kilts.

Plenty of freedom.

Plenty.

dARTS

"If you wanna get good, Bob, three darts are awfully time consuming. It takes about twenty seconds to retrieve three darts, right? Then you've got to throw them again. Three times is about a minute. So, buy three sets of darts. Genius, eh? No wait... that'll take about thirty seconds to retrieve nine darts, won't it? Then you've got to hold them. Okay, so nine darts... right, where was I? Oh, I've lost count. Who cares about darts, anyway?"

"I do, Alex. You want to know what you can count, mate? All the birds you've ever had on one hand."

THE ScANNER

Yvette's mind-numbing job at Asda was made easier by listening to audiobooks through her Bluetooth earpiece. Today, she was on the tills, earpieces were out of the question. To make matters worse, every item she scanned: double beeped.

Her anxiety was through the roof. Her heart was hammering.

Slow, deep breaths, she reminded herself.

Again… beep… beep.

Her fingers began to tingle. Her left arm went numb.

Everything darkened around her.

Beep… beep. That noise. Ugh. Still there.

Slowly, she opened her eyes, head throbbing.

A doctor stood by another bed.

Yvette sighed and closed her eyes.

Beep… beep… beeeeeeeeeeeeep.

FoUNd

The Doc says I have PTSD and I might never be the same again.

I couldn't have wished for anything better.

Mom searches my eyes, touches my cheek, looking unsure.

Dad's been trying to call my phone. My other dad, that is.

He wants his money back. He doesn't want me.

My disappearance has been on the local news, two different incidences in two different states.

The chains and the river worked well. I'm glad about that. They'll never find her.

Now I get the life I deserve.

A new mom and dad.

They shouldn't have separated us at birth.

TRAIN JOURNEYS

I remember the excitement of the unknown: parents falling asleep, kids wandering around. Easier times.

I remember tunnels: staring into the black, waiting for the light to return, reflections to fade.

I remember panic when kids disappeared.

"Where're you heading?" asks an old ticket-inspector in tattered blue.

"Not sure," I say.

He smiles crookedly. "Your conscience knows," he says as the train stops.

Familiar looking boys and girls, ages six, maybe seven, run up the aisle into the next carriage.

There's a clunk. The carriages separate before moving again.

Small faces recede in the window.

The unknown seems less exciting.

WHEELS

Headlights burn into the office from the parking lot.

I'm rolling my thumb along a Zippo wheel.

"Go on, ram it, Stanley. Yeah, you love all that shit, don't you? Ram it right up your fucking arse, mate."

After some threatening sounding revs, Stanley kills the engine, flips open the boot.

Mind games, is it?

He passes the CCTV, swipes his card, and he's in.

"What's that smell?" he says. "Petrol?"

"I'd put that gun away," I say, eyeing the floor. He looks down. "Feels good behind the wheel, doesn't it?" I'm still rolling my thumb. "So, about my wife..."

WAR AND PEACE

Mr. Gomzi, from across the street, was forever shouting at Dad, insisting our dog, Buster, was defecating on his lawn.

"You need to stop arguing with that guy, Dad" I said. "Gonna give yourself a heart attack."

So, Dad comes in, reclines by the fireside "War and peace," he says. At least, I thought he said that.

"You want to read it?" I ask.

"No, no," he says, smiling.

Fire engines, ambulances wail outside.

"What going on out there?"

I look out the window. Mr. Gomzi's house is in flames.

"Warmth and peace," Dad says. And it's clear this time.

ARTY

Throughout Primary School, Arty wore wellies during the summer and gym shoes during the winter. His clothes mirrored his footwear.

Everything was brand new, but his mother had a thing for buying out-of-season goods, and poor Arty got ridiculed for it.

That was until we found out the reason.

She was saving for his little brother's treatment in America. Every penny saved was a penny towards it.

Soon the whole school got involved.

In the summer of 1986, Arty's brother finally got home.

In honour, people lined the street, wearing different-coloured wellies.

I smiled, thinking it looked kind of arty.

SUMMER BREAK

Summer break.

Finally, the boy could write from Monday to Friday without pretending to be ill.

Maybe Mother would spend time in the garden and start reading again, instead of always preparing for those annoying weekend parties: drunks, terrible music, and why did she love to show him off? Ugh, she didn't care.

"Close the laptop. Get out in the sun with your friends," she said.

"But they're all away."

"Out!"

Summer sucked so bad.

He kicked a stone in anger, scratching a line on the path: a letter "I"

He knelt, then he wrote: I hope it doesn't rain.

A WEE CAKE FOR THE ROAD

Dougie was a big guy who liked a wee cake to himself.

He liked other things too, but cakes were the shit.

His excitement went through the roof when he heard a new bakery was opening in two weeks.

The shop was over a mile away.

Perfect, he thought. I can walk to it, burn off some calories, and have a wee cake as a reward.

The first time: the bakery was closed.

Second time: the queue was out the door.

Third time: no cakes left.

Fourth time: forgot his wallet.

There was no fifth time.

He got them delivered.

CEMENTED IN HISTORY

Darren had a reputation for drinking and fighting.

One night, staggering home, he fell face first into wet cement. The weight of his clothes had him stumbling around. The area looked like a well-dug garden.

To avoid further embarrassment, he walked home by the river, tasting the cement, throwing up, convinced he could see carrots in the grey. Why's there always carrots? he wondered. I hate them. Then he caught his reflection.

"Christ, I'm Charlie fucking Chaplin." He laughed.

He lost his balance, fell in.

Two weeks later a fisherman found him.

To this day, his hard-man reputation still stands.

LocKEd AWAY

This large wooden chest contains childhood memories.

The amount of dust reminds me of the beach: swimsuits and tears.

With my sleeve covering my mouth, I flip the latch and open the lid.

More dust invades the attic.

Choking, I stumble back, afraid of what I'll find. Photographs, the truth, days in front of the lens, Uncle Alan putting his hand on my friend Kimberly's shoulder.

That's how it started, how it ended.

I lost all of my friends that year.

Yesterday I spoke to my dad on a telephone behind glass.

He doesn't miss his brother.

He misses me.

THE WEATHER?

"I'm roasting."

"Aye, it's a wee bit muggy outside, son," the shopkeeper says.

Ugh. Small talk. It drives me mental. What is it with people and the weather? I don't answer. He fumbles with my change with his slimy, shaky hands.

Man, get me outta here.

Have you ever noticed when someone says it's clammy, the next person says it's humid, or muggy, sticky, a bit dampish, stuffy even? Like their word is somehow better than yours? I mean fuck sake, no wonder I lose patience.

Now where's best to throw this wallet?

Muggy…. A bit muggy inside more likes.

THE WEATHERMAN

"You wanna know why they call me the Weatherman? I'll tell you. I'm unpredictable. A big spoiler of plans. Think you know me? Know what to expect? You won't see me coming. You don't wanna be inside the belly of the beast. Shit don't come out the same, you see. Ha. You can fly away, sure. You can't escape, though. Day and night don't mean shit. Never has. Plans? Cancel them. Tell everyone you're sorry. Redeem yourself. You're inside a shit storm, sonny. Ha. Sunny. That's a laugh. I'm gonna rip your world apart like a goddamn tornado. Sleep tight."

A Change of Weather

When Aaron's dad said that we shouldn't make faces in case the wind changes because we'd stay like that, I believed him. He knew things. He told Aaron that eating his crusts would make his hair curly. Aaron had the curliest hair in the street.

Anyway, we passed Mr. Whitten's sweet shop, Aaron and I, and saw this little dog lying down, chin pressed to the ground, face all screwed up. When I reached to pat him, a gust of wind knocked me over. He barked. I screamed.

I'd never seen a pug.

I was convinced the wind did it.

IT S GOT TO GO

The sign read:

FREE PERSIAN RUG

"What's wrong with it?" a young man asks.

"Nothing. The wife says I've got to get rid of it."

"Looks a beauty. Getting a new one?"

"Maybe. She says if I don't get rid of that old rug, she's getting rid of me."

"A wee bit over the top, is it not?"

"Yeah, someone else said that."

"Man, this is too nice. I feel like I'm robbing you."

"Nah, you're doing me a favour."

As the man loads the rug into his car, Albert adjusts his hairpiece. "Well, that's the rug gone," he says.

FIT TO BURST

She was on the phone saying: "perfect" and "fit". Things looked promising indeed.

She kept looking at him and smiling. He was biting his lip, thinking about his first poor experience.

She walked over, staring into his eyes. Then she slid her fingers through his hair, brushing it around the back of his ear.

That's when things amplified.

Nervous, excited and afraid, he prayed to God.

There was a chance things would explode any second.

"Relax," she said.

But he couldn't. Nurse or not, the last time his hearing aid was turned up this loud, he almost burst his eardrum.

WE DON'T GIVE UP

I've been stuck in a rut forever, had my soul ripped out. I've been told so many times I don't belong. I've been poked, prodded and stabbed. But it's not in my nature to quit. I keep going.

She came at me, chucking this weird acid-like stuff, yelling "Die scum, die!" I'd never done a thing to her. I thought my time was up.

"Help!" I screamed. "Water!" The whole time she's laughing like a maniac.

But I pushed through, telling myself there was light ahead.

A year has passed. The soil's good. I'm back.

Back peeking through the cracks.

FEELINGS GO

Her face pales.

Her eyes widen, then she backs away.

"You're changing," she says.

I feel confused as I reach for her. I can't move.

My other hand is cuffed to the bed.

I tug and my skin rips from the bone, yet it doesn't hurt.

Why doesn't it hurt?

She raises the axe and stops.

"I don't know if I can," she says, trembling. She looks to the headless child in the corner.

My son.

I reach again, noticing the small bite marks on my hand.

I had no choice. She has no choice.

"Do it," I say. "Please."

WARNING SIGNS

He was always ill, even before breaking his leg playing football. He'd be sick one week, running a fever the next. Sometimes both.

But Jake burning up, while I was at work, is something I have to live with for the rest of my life.

He'd been off school a total of eleven weeks. His friends hadn't visited. He looked depressed.

I didn't realise how much until I found his diary yesterday.

His broken leg wasn't an accident.

The whole school hates me, it read.

Had I known, I wouldn't have let him go to the bonfire with those boys.

THE FIRST DAY OF FALL

(POEM)

A shadow fell over me the first day of fall.

All day I wandered around dazed, feeling hollow.

The weight of waiting for a call, a message, someone saying it's over.

What if they said you were gone? What a terrible thought.

It was the song on the radio that got me. Maybe because I was wasted. Who knows?

I'm not like you: always steady, graceful under grey skies. I know why you lied, your intentions, saying things were fine, that you'd fight.

Please be all right. Please let those shadows disappear inside.

I'm lost without you in my life.

No Worries

My wife takes great pride in putting others first, but sometimes it affects her sleep.

She worries too much.

I didn't want her to worry about me, so I tried dropping a hint.

I bought her a Lion King T-shirt. Hakuna Matata across the front. She sang the song, missed its meaning.

I started whistling "*Don't Worry Be Happy*" to feel better.

"What's up?" she asked.

"Nothing," I said.

She sat beside me, unravelled her earphones, and put one in my ear.

She searched her playlist.

"*A-weema-weh*" faded in.

She sat back and closed her eyes.

Others first as always.

THE LAST FLIGHT

If I listen close, I can hear her breathing above the engines.

She squeezes my hand.

"Are we flying, Nigel?" she asks.

"Always," I tell her.

"Will we fall?"

"Never."

She sighs. "I'd like to stay up here."

"Yeah, me too."

I throw the little brown bottle out of the window into the ocean, trying to ignore the scratchiness in my throat each time I swallow.

"We've always flown together, haven't we, Nigel?"

"Always," I say.

She lets go of my hand, and sighs for the last time. I close my eyes and feel my stomach drop.

We're not falling.

ACKNOWLEDGMENTS:

Thank you to Liz, Joe, Katie, Mum, Dad and my sister, Tracey. Jennifer Bernardini and Sarah Frost for their edits and suggestions, Leanne Clydesdale for her encouragement, Edward Lorn, Chad Lutzke, Kevin Whitten, George Ranson, Steven Gomzi, Kami Martin, Aaron Nash, Steve Vassallo, Brad Proctor, Max Stark, J.B. Taylor and all the other good folks on Twitter who help to make my day a little brighter.

Thanks for reading.

Hope you had some fun.

Love

Wayne.

Printed in Great Britain
by Amazon

46050181R00076